I is not understanding what this is

Library of Congress Cataloging-in-Publication Data available

ISBN 978-0-545-69466-7

10 9 8 7 6 5 4 3 2 1   15 16 17 18 19

Printed in China 84
First American edition, May 2015

Book design by Ellen Duda

This diary is

TOP SECRET

keep
out !!!

(especially if you)
is evil

Me I is Pig. I is 465 sunsets old, but every day I gets older, so this fact is only correct right now, on the day I is writing.

I live in Pig House. Pig House is next to **CHICKEN HOUSE**, which is across from **COW shed**, which is not too far from **Duck Pond**.

I has drawn a map for you

Duck Pond

The New Barn

The Old Hay Barn

I is the only Pig that lives here. I has only ever been called Pig, so Pig is my name.

this is me. I is Pig!

I is a very lucky Pig. Of all the animals in the yard I thinks that **Farmer** loves me most 'cause he always gives me lots of yummy slops and lots of special back scratches. I loves back scratches but most of all I LOVES yummy slops. Yummy sloppy food. I loves my food. I dream about food A LOT.

Mushy parsnips, mashed-up carrots, sloppy potatoes... See? When I gets going it's ALL I can thinks about.

Anyways, what I bet you is wondering is what is a Pig doing writing a diary. Well it's simple, really. I often goes sniffing around the garbage cans that **Farmer** leaves out by the main gate. I goes snuffling in 'em to see if I can find more slops. But today I didn't find no slops or scraps, I found this little book and a very chewed old pen, and I thoughts to myself, wouldn't it be fun to keep a diary. I is not sure who will be reading this diary, but I is thinking whoever you is you must be very clever 'cause you can read Pig! Or maybe you is a Pig too—who knows.

Anyways, here goes:

unbelievable

The ⋀ top secret diary of Pig

Scholastic Press / New York

Day 1

(I has no idea what to call this day, so as it is the first day I is writing this diary, I will call it DAY 1. And then it will be simple after that. You will see.)

Hello.

Today I is very happy! **Farmer** gave me two big dollops of slops. I ate them all very fast and they made me windy. **Farmer** let me out into the yard, so I went straight over towards the

CHICKEN HOUSE and laid some big fat farts right next to it.

I is really not liking **CHICKENS**. They is evil. I is sure if you was to meet them you would think they is evil too. **EVIL CHICKENS** is evil because:

1. When I is not looking they sticks their evil beaks into my bowl and eats my slops. If I shouts at them to stop, they pecks me on my head. They has nasty sharp evil beaks and it hurts.

2. When **COW** lies down to sleep, they hops on her back and does little poos all

over her. They thinks this is very funny. I thinks this is very nasty. I wish **COW** wasn't so nice and would poo on them.

3. They steals my friend **Duck's** special **Duck** food. **Farmer** gives it to him in a bowl, but as soon as **Farmer** isn't looking the **EVIL CHICKENS** push **Duck** out of the way and eat it. **Duck** pretends that he doesn't care, but I knows deep down inside he does.

4. They has nasty evil little eyes. They is very black. Like little dark holes that is made of pure evil! I is not liking their evil little eyes,

I hates evil chickens

they makes me feel scared just looking
at them.

Once I had finished stinking up the
CHICKEN HOUSE, I went over to
see **Duck**. **Duck** is great. I
likes **Duck** very, very much.
If you met **Duck** I knows you
would like him too.

There used to be more than one **Duck**,
but one night **Fox** came and ate
them all up.

Fox ate **Duck's** mum,
his dad, and all his
brothers and sisters.
Fox is very nasty. He
made **Duck** very sad.

5

I knows what it is like not to have a mum or dad or brothers and sisters 'cause I got taken away from mine when I was very little and brought here to live with **Farmer**. So I made an extra-special effort to cheer **Duck** up. Me and **Duck** is best friends now. **Duck** says I is like a brother, only I don't have feathers or funny flappy feet. Ha! Ha! **Duck** always makes me laugh.

Duck lives in a little shed in the middle of **Duck Pond**. That way **Fox** can't get him 'cause **Fox** can't swim. Ha! Ha! **Mr. Fox** is not so clever now!

Duck is very clever. He speaks lots of languages. He speaks: Pig, **CHICKEN**, **COW**, Sheep, and **Farmer**. This is much better

than I can do. I can only speak **Duck** (it's
a lot like Pig—just listen to the noise
of a **Duck** talking and the noise of a Pig
talking, and you will sees what I mean).
And I speaks a little bit of **COW** and
Sheep. I can't speak any **Farmer**, but
I can understand a teensy-weensy bit
if I listens really hard and concentrates. I
hopes that you can read Pig otherwise
you won't be able to understands a word
that I is writing. Ha! Ha!

I can't swim, so I sits on the side with
my trotters in the mud and waits for
Duck to come over.

Today **Duck** told me that he thinks the
EVIL CHICKENS are planning something. He says
that last night they were up very late in

the **CHICKEN HOUSE**. Way past lights-out.
He said they didn't come and steal his food
today either, which means they must be
up to something, 'cause they always make
time to steal his food.

yummy cabbyage

Duck told me I should eat
less. He says that way I will
live longer. But I says if I don't
eat so much then I will
shrink right down and be a
Mini-Pig. **Duck** says if I is
small **Farmer** will keep
me longer. But **Farmer**
is very happy when
I eat. **Duck** is silly
sometimes.

At the end of the day **Farmer** came and put me back into Pig House. He gave me one of his special back scratches and made a very happy noise. **Farmer** likes me big. **Duck** is so wrong.

yummy carrot

I is going to make myself as big as I can. That way **Farmer** will love me more.

Day 2

Hello.

Today was very BORING! It was so BORING that I shall only write a very small amount, so as I doesn't make you BORED too.

Today **Farmer** gave me two helpings of slops. This was NOT boring. This was very exciting.

But then it rained.

I ♡ yummy slops

Farmer didn't let me out in the yard, so I just watched **Duck** having fun in his pond and wished that I could swim like him. If I could swim, I would swim around and around the pond. First on my front and then on my back. And then I would build a big platform and jump off it, doing all kinds of somersaults in the air.

But I can't use a hammer, so I can't build a platform and I can't swims neither. So that is the end of that. BORING.

Day 3

Hello.

It's stopped raining. HOORAY!

The yard is very muddy. HOORAY! HOORAY!

Farmer gave me three helpings of slops. HOORAY! HOORAY! HOORAY!

Farmer looked very happy that I ate all my three helpings. He scratched my back and called me by my special name, Roast Pig. I has no idea what it means, but it sounds nice when he says it. I tells **Duck** about my special name. He says it is not special. I thinks he says this 'cause he is jealous that **Farmer** doesn't have names for him.

Farmer is great. Every morning he is giving me back scratches and special rubs behind my ears and patting my tummy. I wish I could scratch **Farmer's** back and rub him behind his ears to show him that I love him back.

After my breakfast I was so full that my belly was nearly touching the floor. Boy, oh boy, more BIG FARTS. I went and sat

on the edge of **Duck Pond** and did some
and they went bubble, bubble, bubble, and
me and **Duck** laughed A LOT. **Duck** said it
was like swimming in a smelly hot tub.

I saw the EVIL CHICKENS watching. I think
they were jealous of me and **Duck** having
fun. EVIL CHICKENS don't do fun. They just do
stealing everyone's food and pooing on **COW**.
Oh, and they also do laying eggs. I think that
these is probably evil too. But **Farmer**
and **Mrs. Farmer** seems to like them
very much. They built the EVIL CHICKENS
a special house, with a special door that
stops **Fox** from coming in and eating them
all up like he did the **Ducks**. **Fox** is the only
thing that the EVIL CHICKENS is scared of.

After I had finished in the pond, I went
over and played in my special bit of mud
that only I play in. It's just next to the
Sheep Field.

Nobody else knows it is there, apart
from the **Sheep** of course. But **Sheep** don't
do rolling in mud, 'cause they're too silly to
realize
how fun
rolling in
mud is.
They just
stands
there and
watches
me, their

funny heads following me as I roll around and around.

Rolling in mud is fun, fun, fun! Give it a try if you likes. Just find a big old patch of mud and jump right in and squelch around and around. It feels so good, especially when it is really thick mud and it sticks everywhere.

Duck says that after I have been rolling around in mud I looks like a chocolate Pig. Ha! Ha! **Duck** is very funny!

Then I watched **Farmer** milking **COW**. Like I says before, I don't speaks much **COW** and **COW** only

speaks a tiny bit of Pig, so we don't say too much to each other. And when **COW** does say stuff, sometimes it don't make no sense at all. But I say nothing about it making no sense, 'cause that would be rude.

Today **COW** says to me, **"hello, pig, you look very turnip."**

I think she means **"happy,"** 'cause in Pig "happy" and "turnip" sound very similar. I think this is probably because turnips and happiness are pretty much the same to Pigs. I LOVES TURNIPS.

So I says to **COW**, so as not to be rude, "Yes, I is very turnip today, thank you."

Farmer gave me a slurp of **COW'S** milk. Oh, boy, it was soooooo yummy! If I could milk **COW** myself, I would be in heaven. In fact, even betters, I would be a **COW** and then I would be able to milk myself all day long. Only I would have to be a **COW** with very bendy legs, so as they could bend around and touch my udders.

Hmmmm, why don't Pigs have udders like **COWS**? That would be AMAZING!

Farmer and **Mrs. Farmer** came to see me tonight. They both gave me big back scratches. And **Mrs. Farmer** measured

my middle with a long piece of tape. She looked very happy. **Farmer** called me by my special name again and **Mrs. Farmer** said, **"Mmm . . . sausages."** What a silly sounding words that is. Saus-ages, saus-ages. Ha! Ha! Ha! I think **Mrs. Farmer** likes me too.

Day 4

Hello.

You will be SO glad I is writing this diary for you, because today **Duck** told me some very amazing news:

THE **EVIL CHICKENS** IS BUILDING A SPACE ROCKET!!!!!

Duck said he heard them talking about it last night. He sneaked up and listened right outside the door of **CHICKEN HOUSE**. They have drawn up plans and everything. Big plans. They is building it

out of the broken tractor in the Old Hay Barn.

I can't believe it. **Duck** says that they have been building it for ages and no one has noticed 'cause no one goes in the Old Hay Barn 'cause no one would want to go in there but the **EVIL CHICKENS** 'cause it is dark and smells yucky. They go in there and pretend to scratch around, while all the time what they is really doing is building a SPACE ROCKET!

Oh, and **Duck** told me again that I should stop eating so much. He says I look nearly ready for the "pot." He won't tell me what the "pot" is. He just says it is bad. I say that the "pot" sounds nice. Sounds like something you keep lots of yummy food in.

Yum-diddly-scrumptious. **Duck** says I is silly. I say **Duck** is silly. Silly, silly, silly!

Anyways, this afternoon I sneaked over towards the Old Hay Barn to see what the **EVIL CHICKENS** had built. I was super sneaky. I turned myself into a pile of hay. Covered myself from head to toe in it, I did. 'Cause if I had just walked over dressed as Pig they would have spotted me straight away. But it wasn't as totally sneaky as I had hoped, 'cause a bit of hay tickled my nose and, just as I got near the barn, I sneezed really hard and all the hay dropped off. One of the **EVIL CHICKENS** poked his head out to see what was going on, so I quickly pretended to be looking for yummy worms to eat in the mud. Ha! Ha! Pig fooled you, **EVIL CHICKEN!**

Tomorrow I is going to make a better disguise. Tomorrow I is going to go as a big heap of poo!!! I is so excited I can hardly sleep.

I LOVES space rockets, they is just so big and exciting. Imagine riding one around in the sky!!! But I don't loves them as much as slops and **Farmer**. I don't love anything more than I loves slops and **Farmer**.

Day 5

Hello.

I really smells BAD. I smells of poo. Yuck, yuck. If you was here right now you would be holding your nose and saying, "Phooooey, you reeks of poo, Pig!"

I smells bad because all day I have been pretending to be a heap of poo. I cannot

 tells you how hard it is being a heap of poo. You should try it. Actually, no you shouldn't.

You probably smell all nice and soapy. It would be a shame if you smelled of poo.

It is hard being a heap of poo because:

1. Poo is heavier than you think and it is very hard to walk covered in it.

2. Poo gets in your eyes and makes it hard for you to see.

3. Poo attracts lots of flies, so wherever you go there is a loud buzzing sound in your ears.

4. Poo smells of poo and that is a BAD smell.

I covered myself in poo from the big poo heap. You should see it—it is huge! **Farmer** adds more poo to it every day until it is as big as a mountain, and then he spreads it all over his fields. **Duck** says the poo has special powers that make the grass grow even faster. Magic poo.

Ha! Ha! Ha!

Once I had finished covering myself,
I shuffled off towards the Old Hay Barn. I
went really slowly, crawling so they couldn't
see my legs. I tucked my ears in and

 stuffed a large piece
of old cow poo on my
tail, so they couldn't
see those neither.

It took me sooo long to get across the yard
that when I finally got to the Old Hay Barn
it was dark and I couldn't see inside.

So I smells of poo for NOTHING!!
Farmer couldn't understand what had
happened. He washed me down with a giant
hose, but he couldn't get all the poo off so
I still smells BAD.

But even though I really reek he gave me a special extra portion of slops, a super big back scratch, and a long rub behind the ear. He is my bestest friend.

Well, him and **Duck** are my bestest friends. But **Duck** doesn't give me slops and back scratches, so if I is honest, I is loving **Farmer** a teeny-tiny bit more. But please don't be telling that to **Duck**.

Day 6

Hello.

You WILL NOT believe what has happened today. I don't believe what happened today and it happened TO ME.

It all started after breakfast.

Like normal, I went out, laid a big fat fart outside the **EVIL CHICKEN HOUSE** (today it was a proper stinker—it even made me want to hold my nose), and then I went to see **Duck** and play by the pond.

Only, when I gets to the pond one of the **EVIL CHICKENS** is there too. It was the Super Evil one. The one that is pecking me on the head the hardest when I is complaining about them stealing my slops. Pure **SUPER EVIL CHICKEN!**

I is just about to head back to Pig House when **Duck** says to me that **SUPER EVIL CHICKEN** wants a word about their little secret. I pretend like I don't give a lump o' chicken poop what it has to say, but inside I is really as curious as a rat in a corn shed.

The **EVIL CHICKENS** speak Pig, but they speak it very slowly and very loudly with a silly posh-sounding accent. I has trouble listening to it without giggling. But I try not to laugh, because I really want to know about their secret.

ONE KNOWS HOW VERY MUCH YOU WOULD LIKE TO SEE OUR SECRET PROJECT. SO IF YOU WILL KINDLY FOLLOW ME, ONE WILL SHOW YOU,

says the **SUPER EVIL CHICKEN**.
How does he know how much I
want to see their secret
project? I was super sneaky
with my disguises. He must be
talking about **Duck**, I thinks.
But I don't say nothing, 'cause
I don't want to make **Duck**
look silly.

Me and **Duck** follows **SUPER EVIL
CHICKEN** into the Old Hay Barn and there it
is in front of our very eyes. It's ginormous.
If only you could see it. It looks like a

cross between a tractor and a rocket, like a Trocket. (Ha! Ha! I is funny.)

Anyways, it was so stupendous that my eyes nearly popped out of my head—pop, pop! And it doesn't need any fancy fuel to make it work. It uses poo!!! (**Duck** was right, poo really is magic.) But most amazing of all is that they is going to fly it to PLUTO!!!!!!!!!!

"Why Pluto?" I says. They says they has to go to Pluto to beat the record set by the **CHICKENS** in the farm across the valley.

Turns out that last year the **EVIL CHICKENS** across the valley built a Trocket of their own and sent it to Mars. And you really won't be believing this—the pilot was a Pig! The **SUPER EVIL CHICKEN** says that Pigs make the best pilots 'cause they is super brave and fearless. When I is hearing this I is feeling very proud inside and also a little confused. I is not sure why the **EVIL CHICKENS** is suddenly being so nice.

The **EVIL CHICKENS** here has even built their own telescope, out of an old drainpipe, so

that they can take pictures of their Trocket when it reaches Pluto, and show the EVIL CHICKENS across the valley how clever they is.

The SUPER EVIL CHICKEN says that the Trocket is almost complete and that all they needs is an astronaut to fly it. Then the SUPER EVIL CHICKEN says the most AMAZING, AMAZING thing.

It says they wants me to be the one who flies it. Me, Astronaut Pig, flying to Pluto. Can you believe it?

But of course I can't go, that would be silly. Who would feed me slops on Pluto? And there is not enough space for **Farmer** and me in the Trocket.

I tells the SUPER EVIL CHICKEN thank you, but no thank you. **Farmer** loves me very much. I could never leave him.

The **SUPER EVIL CHICKEN** just laughs at me and says that I will find out just how much **Farmer** loves me very, very soon. I is thinking this sounds like a lovely thing. But the way **SUPER EVIL CHICKEN** says it, it sounds bad. Only the **EVIL CHICKENS** could make something nice sound horrible.

Farmer gave me five portions of slops today. He called me my special name again, Roast Pig, and said I was nearly ready.

I think "nearly ready" means something is going to happen soon. I hope more slops is going to happen soon.

How exciting. I love **Farmer** soooo much.

Day 7

Hello.

Today has been the worst day of my life. So bad that it has made my heart ache really badly. I is wondering if it may actually be broken up into tiny little pieces.

Today is a bad day, because today I found out, **Farmer** DOESN'T LOVE ME— HE WANTS TO EAT ME FOR HIS DINNER!

I wish that I had never gone over to see **Duck** after slops, because if I hadn't, I would never have had to know. But then if I never did know, I think that might have been even worse.

So, today **Farmer** gave me more slops than ever before and I can hardly walk. In fact I is so tired after I have eaten that I don't even go out in the yard. I just lie around in my shed. I is just about to fall asleep and have big dreams about more slops when **Duck** waddles in and says he has something important to show

me and that I must go with him to
Farmer's Shed. Farmer's Shed is
over in the far corner and only **Farmer**
ever goes there. So I have no idea why
Duck wants us to go.

As we gets closer I sees on the door that

Farmer has nailed a golden square of
metal with a picture of a sad-faced big
fat Pig scratched into it. Looking at it

gives me funny goose bumps all over. **Duck**
nudges open the door and we goes inside. In
the middle there is this big wooden table,
some large hooks hanging from the ceiling,
and a big ax. It doesn't smell nice in there
neither and I tell **Duck** I don't like it. **Duck**
says I shouldn't like it.

Then he tells me the worst thing in the
world I have ever heard. He says that this
is where **Farmer** kills his Pigs. And I says,
"Don't be silly, Farmer doesn't have any Pigs,
he just has me." And **Duck** says, **"Yup, that's
right, you are the Pig he is going to kill, Pig."**

Apparently **Farmer** has had many Pigs
like me and they has all come in here and
they has all never come out.

He showed me this chart on the wall, which gives **Farmer** instructions on

how to cut me up into lots of different pieces. I felt sick, sick to my very stomach. So I ran straight back to my shed and I stuck my trotters in my ears so I couldn't hear any more bad ever again. And this is when I think my heart snapped in two, or maybe three or maybe four. It really hurt.

I was thinking **Farmer** loved me. I was thinking I was his bestest Pig. All that time he was feeding me and scratching me and

patting me, he was thinking about
EATING ME!

Farmer doesn't love me! I don't love
Farmer!

Farmer wants to eat me! I wish I
could eat **Farmer** instead!!

Duck came back in and he said that
he was sorry he told me, but he thought
maybe I should know and that, just maybe,
I should think about taking up the EVIL
CHICKENS' offer and going to Pluto. Because
if I was on Pluto, there was no way
Farmer could chop me up and eat me
for his dinner.

I said I would
think about it.

Day 8

Hello.

This has been the second-worst day of my life. Can you believe it? Two bad days in a row. Very unfair.

When **Farmer** came over this morning to feed me, I gave him my evilest stare. It was so evil I reckon even the **EVIL CHICKENS** couldn't have done better. But **Farmer** just patted me even more. He tried to give me a scratch behind the ear, but I moved my head away quickly and I shouted as loud as I could, "DON'T TOUCH ME,

evil
← lemon

YOU EVIL LEMON!!!" (Lemon is a really bad word in Pig, 'cause Pigs HATE lemons. They taste bad, bad, bad.)

But **Farmer** doesn't understand a word of what I has said. He just laughs and says, "Oink, oink" and rubs my head. I is so wishing I could talk to **Farmer** and tell him how much I HATE HIM.

I has decided that if **Farmer** wants me big, then I shall make myself small. So I only eats some of my slops. I has to eat a little bit though, 'cause I LOVES them so much. Boy, oh boy, it was very difficult to do—I has NEVER not eaten all my slops.

Farmer left me and went off to milk

COW, so I snuck out and went to see **Duck**.

And **Duck** said he had something else to tell me. I said if it was BAD, I didn't want to hear it. And he said it was BAD, but he was going to tell me anyway. **Duck** is so mean sometimes.

Duck says he overheard SUPER EVIL CHICKEN talking with another EVIL CHICKEN.

Apparently, EVIL CHICKENS like putting Pigs in their Trockets not because they are brave and fearless, but because they are

"EXPENDABLE." I says to **Duck** I have no idea what "expendable" is. So he tells me. "Expendable" means that if the Trocket goes bang in a puff of smoke or flies off into space and is never seen again, then no one will miss me. I pretends like this doesn't bother me, like I don't care if no one would miss me. I has to pretend very hard though and I has to keep rubbing my eyes, as they keeps filling up with tears.

    Duck says this isn't true, that he would miss me. I LOVE **Duck** sometimes. (I take back the bit where I said that I loved **Farmer** a teeny-tiny bit more than **Duck**. I loves **Duck** soooo much more. I was so silly!)

I told you the **EVIL CHICKENS** is Pure Evil.
I is Pig the Expendable.

What would you do if you was me? I
don't want to be eaten by **Farmer**.
I don't want to shoot off into space and
explode in a massive fireball with bits of
me flying off across
the big black sky
willy-nilly, or
just end up
lost forever,
floating around
all on my own.

I think my heart may just have broken
into even more pieces. I can't write any
more. I is too sad.

Day 9

Hello.

I woke up hoping that all of this was just a big bad dream and that **Farmer** didn't really want to eat me, and that the EVIL CHICKENS didn't really want to use me as their Expendable Pig Pilot.

But then **Farmer** comes over with my slops and he brings **Mrs. Farmer** and she brings the tape measure again. She puts it around my tummy.

I is not silly though. This time I sucks my tummy in as hard as I can, to try and make myself mini. I holds my breath for so long I nearly falls over. But I don't think my plan works, 'cause **Mrs. Farmer** turns to **Farmer** and nods and says, **"Nearly ready"** and now I know what this means. It means NEARLY READY TO BE CHIP-CHOPPED UP IN **Farmer's Shed**!

I feels so sick inside that even though I is super-duper hungry, I don't even want my slops. So I sticks my nose in them and

 *Wink! Wink!* make some slurpy noises, but I don't eat any at all. **Farmer** says, **"That's right, eat up, my Special Pig."**

Ha! Ha! Stupid **Farmer**. I is not your Special Pig and I is not eating ANYTHING!!

But though I is pretending to be all hard on the outside, I is not feeling all hard on the inside. So I cries a little bit, but I does it behind the Old Hay Barn so no one can see me and think I is a Big Softie Pig. Then I comes to a decision, just like that.

I IS GOING TO PLUTO!

I is going to take my chances in outer space. If I dies in a big explosion or gets lost forever, then at least **Farmer** and **Mrs. Farmer** won't be able to eat me.

So I goes and sees **Duck** and I tells him to tell the **EVIL CHICKENS**. I will be their astronaut. I is brave. I is fearless. I is Pig.

And Pig is off to PLUTO!!!

Day 10

Hello.

Last night the **SUPER EVIL CHICKEN** came around and told me what the next steps of the plans are. I has to hand it to the **EVIL CHICKENS**. They is EVIL, but they is smart as haystacks too.

They has built a pipe from my slops trough to the Old Hay Barn, and every day they is going to drain all the slops I don't eat into a tank in the Trocket, so that I will have enough food to last the journey. The less slops I eat now, the more slops I will have on my journey.

They says that in a couple of days' time they thinks they will have enough slops for me and I should prepare myself to leave on the night of the small moon. That ways, they says, there will be the least chance of any **Farmer** spotting the Trocket and sending Fighter Planes to shoot it down.

FIGHTER PLANES TO SHOOT IT DOWN?!

I asks **Duck** what Fighter Planes are. He says I really don't want to know. I thinks he is right. I don't want to fill my head up with any more bad stuff. If I gets any more scared I thinks I will shake so much I won't be able to write my diary for you.

Today I only eats five mouthfuls of slops (just enough so my tummy doesn't rumble too much) and the rest disappears into the pipe.

I had saved up all my farts from yesterday, so when **Farmer** leaned over my door to pour the slops into my trough, I let out the biggest most stinky fart I has ever done. It made him cough really badly and hold his nose.

Ha! Ha! **Farmer** eat my stinky fart!

Then I went and saw **Duck**. I is pretending not to be scared, but inside I is a whole big bag of butterflies and all other kinds of fluttery stuff. **Duck** says that it will all be all right. He also says to remember that the EVIL CHICKENS has a telescope, so I can wave back to everyone and I won't have to feel so alone.

I has no idea how I is going to find my way to Pluto. I hope the EVIL CHICKENS has a map.

Day 11

Hello.

This morning the **EVIL CHICKENS** took me to the **Sheep Barn** and weighed me in **Farmer's** special weighing machine. They says they need to know my weight so they can make some calculations. They

says I weighs a lot. They is so rude! I is a Pig; I is meant to weigh a lot. But they has the Trocket and I needs the Trocket, so I says nothing about their rudeness.

They says me being so heavy is a bit of a problem 'cause the Trocket needs to be super light for takeoff. So to lighten the load they is only going to fill the fuel tank half-full. I is going to have to make the rest of the poo myself as I flies along.

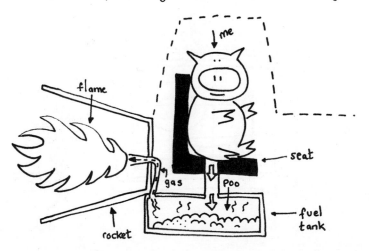

They has built a special tube that goes from under my seat to the fuel tank. All I has to do is keep eating and keep pooing and the Trocket will keep flying.

After my weighing I spent the rest of the day doing things that I won't be able to do no more when I is in space.

I itched my back eight times on the iron gate.

I did three big monster farts in **Duck Pond**. They was so big they made him bob up and down in the water.

I rolled around in my special area of mud that only I roll in next to the **Sheep Field**.

I went over to **COW** and had the Turnip Conversation again.

I told **Duck** that I would miss him, 'cause I will. But not in a softie way.

And finally, I pressed my bum up against the wood panels of **CHICKEN HOUSE** and did one super-evil-grade-A fart just as they was getting ready for bedtime.

Day 12

Hello.

Today is my last day on the farm and on Earth. Tonight I is leaving. And I is writing my diary to you in the afternoon, 'cause by nighttime I will be getting into the Trocket, ready for blastoff.

Today I can hardly thinks at all, 'cause my head is full up with the words...

They go around and around, over and over, so there is no room for anything else. I didn't even have space in my head to think about doing any farting. I just spent the day walking around and around my shed. **Farmer** looked at me very strange.

And now the sun is setting so it is almost time for me to go to the Old Hay Barn. These might be my very last writings ever. I is hoping very much that they isn't. I shall sneak my diary into the Trocket and take it with me. That way if I is not splatted across the sky or shot down by Fighter Planes, I can tell you what happens.

Good-bye for now, hopefully not forever.

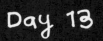

Day 13

BOOM!

I is dead!!

HA! HA!
Only joking!

I is ALIVE!

And I is rocketing towards Pluto as I writes. I bet you is wondering how it all went yesterday. So I will fill you in.

Just after sunset I walked over to the Old Hay Barn. All the EVIL CHICKENS was inside. They had made a huge hole in the roof so the Trocket could fly out.

The EVIL CHICKENS shows me around the Trocket. They has made me a seat from the old tractor one. I has a seat belt made from this thing that they says is called a "fan belt." I has a steering wheel, a brake, and a speedometer, which is a thing showing how fast I is going. I also has something that is called a "sat nav." It is a special thing that talks to **Farmers** in their cars so they knows where they is going. The **EVIL CHICKENS** has stolen it from **Farmer's** car and changed it so that it speaks in Pig, not **Farmer**. I just has to follow the instructions it gives me. I don't have to do much, I just has to remember to brake when I gets to Pluto, otherwise I will crash right into it! They has also stuck **Farmer's** toolbox on the side—they says this is just in case I has any problems I needs to fix. I thinks they says this to make me feel better, but it just makes me feel more scared. I is not knowing how to fix any problems even if I has a toolbox.

Finally they shows me the most important thing—a special tube that I sucks on when

I wants slops. But I must be careful and not eat all my slops at once. I is worried about this. I LOVES SLOPS!

I says a final good-bye to **Duck** (even **COW** comes over to watch). I want to hug **Duck**, but I can't because I don't want him to think I is a Softie Pig. On the inside I is feeling more scared than I has ever felt ever before.

I climbs into the Trocket and even though I is shaking A LOT I manages to cleverly sneak my diary and pen with me, and I hide them under my bottom so I can still write to you even when I is far, far away in space.

The **SUPER EVIL CHICKEN** presses the green GO button on the side of the Trocket and it roars into life. Suddenly I remembers a very important question that I has forgotten all along. I is so silly! What do I do if I gets there and I don't like it and there are no slops?

I shouts this question down to the **EVIL CHICKENS**, but I guess they doesn't hear, 'cause they just happily waves at me with their **EVIL CHICKEN** wings as I rocket up into the sky.

Takeoff was very loud and smelly. Burning poo smells super bad. I just crossed my trotters and closed my eyes, and when I opened them again I looked out of the window and Earth was so small it looked like a pea in some thick dark slops.

The Trocket goes very, very fast. It goes so fast that it feels like someone is pulling my cheeks back. It makes it hard to eat my slops, which is a good thing really, otherwise I thinks I might eat them all at once.

I whizzes past the moon so fast that I doesn't even have a chance to see if it is really made of cheese like **Duck** told me. I is suspecting that it is not, because if it was, then surely some **Mice** would have built a Mouse Rocket and come and eaten it all.

Space is very black. I has never seen anything so black in all my life. It is blacker than the black I sees when I closes my eyes at night. It is even blacker than the eyes of the **EVIL CHICKENS**.

I hopes that I don't have to spend too much time in space. I don't like it very much and I don't have **Duck** here with me to tell me that it is going to be OK. I miss him very much. I wishes now I had told him how much I loves him rather than pretending to be all tough and brave. I is such a silly Pig sometimes.

Fazzleday

Hello.

First of all, I must be explaining the funny day name. It is always dark in space. The sun doesn't come up or go down, which means I has no idea when one day stops and another one starts. So I has had an idea. I is going to invent my own days. They will be as long and as short as I likes and they will have their own special names. I likes this idea very much.

I has got used to the smell of burning poo, so I don't have to hold my nose anymore. This is a very good thing, let me tell you,

'cause holding my nose all the time was making my trotter ache.

I imagines what **Farmer** will be thinking back down there on Earth. I wonder if he is looking for me. Ha! Ha! I is not there anymore. Silly **Farmer**, he will never find me, ever, ever.

I is trying very hard not to think about what will happen if there is no slops on Pluto. This would be very bad. But I still thinks that being chip-chopped up by **Farmer** would be worse. So I thinks positive thoughts. Even if there is only boring hay there, that wouldn't be so bad. Well, it would be. I is just trying to pretend.

The sat nav is very rude. The **EVIL CHICKENS** has changed all the words to Pig, but they has done it themselves, so I is being given directions in Picken. (Pig words spoken by **CHICKENS**. Ha! Ha! I is still very funny even in space!) The Picken voice says to me, "CONGRATULATIONS, OLD BEAN, YOU ARE NOW APPROACHING THE PLANET JUPITER. PLEASE DO MAKE A U-TURN AND CONTINUE STRAIGHT FOR ANOTHER TWELVE THOUSAND MILES, YOU UTTERLY RIDICULOUS, SILLY, SMELLY PIGGY."

Then I hears them all starts laughing their horrible evil laugh, "KLA! KLA! KLA! KLA!"

I hates the CHICKENS so much. But I is too busy being an astronaut to let them bother me.

I is not really sure what a "you turn" is, so I just steers the wheel the way the arrow points on screen. I thinks I can see Pluto. It is a small white dot. But there is

lots of small white dots, so I is not really that sure.

I really hopes the sat nav is right, 'cause I is getting a little bored. Well, that is not true. I is getting a lot bored. Even making farts is getting boring with no one around to smell them. I tried to play I Spy, but it is hard when there is just one of you, 'cause you always know the answer: star, planet, dashboard, belly, steering wheel, or slops.

I is starting to get a little worried about my slops too. When I sucks on the pipe, it is starting to make a kind of slurping noise, like when something starts to run out. I is really crossing all my trotters that there is something tasty for me to eat on Pluto.

Wongleday

Hello.

Panic, panic, panic!!!

I sadly has to report that I is all out of slops, and as I has no slops, I has no way of making poo. So I has run out of fuel too. I is now floating through space. I think I can see Pluto ahead of me. It's a funny blue-green color. I is really hoping that I is going to land on it and not float right on past it into outer, outer space.

The **Picken** sat nav says to me, "MY DEAR FELLOW, YOU HAVE SO VERY NEARLY REACHED THE FINAL DESTINATION. HUZZAH! WE ARE WISHING YOU A VERY PLEASANT LANDING. PLEASE DO BE CAREFUL NOT TO CRASH AND DIE IN A HORRENDOUS BIG BALL OF FLAMES. KLA! KLA! KLA! KLA!"

I is super scared. It is hard to write this 'cause I is shaking quite a bit.

I is wishing **Duck** was here with me to say something funny or even just to tell me that it is all going to be OK. All the lights has gone out in the Trocket, so I can't play I Spy even if I wanted to, 'cause now

all I can spy is
black.

Once again, I
is getting the
feeling inside like
I is wanting to cry
a bit, like a Big
Softie Pig. But
there is no one up here who would be able
to say, "It's OK, Pig, don't cry," so there
don't seem no point. I will keep all my tears
in for now. When I gets super thirsty I
might needs them to drink anyways.

Please, please, let it be all OK. I don't
wants to be lost in space forever without
no slops.

Dibbleday

Wooo-hoo!

Hello! I is really not sure you will be believing what happened today!

Today I has landed the Trocket on Pluto. I really is a Pig Astronaut. Though I has to say I would have crashed into it if I had not woken myself up with my very loud snoring. I opened my eyes and right there in front of me was Pluto. I turned the wheel around as hard as I could so the Trocket landed on its bottom rather than on its nose.

I is landing at nighttime, so it is hard to see what Pluto is like. I presses my face against the window to try and see, but it is just too dark and all I can see is my own Pig face staring back at me. I is not sure I really wants to go outside. I is not really liking the dark very much, and I is even less liking the dark when I has no idea what is in it!

But I has no choice. There is no food left in the Trocket and I is starting to get hungry. I has to go outside and see what is out there. So I takes a deep breath and I opens the Trocket door.

I steps out and there, standing right in front of me, is a **SPACE ALIEN**.

A **SPACE ALIEN**!

I is so shocked I does a little jump back

and at the same time I does a little surprised fart. The **SPACE ALIEN** must be as shocked as I is, 'cause it don't say a word about me or my fart. It just stands there as still as a stone, looking at me. I hopes that maybe it didn't hear my fart. I is thinking it is not very polite to be farting the first time you meet someone new.

The **SPACE ALIEN** was the strangest-looking thing. It looked a bit like **Farmer**—if you shrunk **Farmer** to the size of a **CHICKEN**, made him fat, and gave him a hairy face and a pointy hat.

"Hello," I says. "My name is Pig. What is yours?"

I is guessing that it was not understanding Pig 'cause it says nothing.

As my eyes gets used to looking in the dark, I sees there is whole lot more **SPACE ALIENS** all standing looking at me. Some is holding little sticks in their hands and

one is holding a thing that looks like a space wheelbarrow. It's just like the wheelbarrow that **Farmer** uses in the yard, only much, much smaller.

I is starting to feel a little scared, but I is determined to be

brave, so I says
hello again, only
this time I says it
a bit louder so
they can all hear.
And just in case
none of them can
understand I
waves as well.

But they all says nothing. They just
stands there and stares straight at me
with their small black eyes. Their eyes is
just like the EVIL CHICKENS' eyes, I thinks, and
then I thinks a terrible thought. What if
they is evil just like the CHICKENS? What
if they is EVIL SPACE ALIENS and they is

not saying anything 'cause their brains is all too busy thinking about the nasty things they is going to do to me? I quickly jumps back in the Trocket and shuts the door.

I sits in the Trocket all by myself and suddenly feels very lonely and scared. I is not sure that Pluto is a very nice place. I is not sure the **SPACE ALIENS** is very nice. I really, really wishes **Duck** was here

with me. And then the most amazing thing happened. I closes my eyes as tightly as I can and thinks about **Duck** in my head.

I imagines that I is
sitting on the edge
of **Duck Pond** having
one of our chats.
"Hello, **Duck**," I says
"What are you up to?"

And **Duck** replies in my head, "**Um huck
in he hool hox**."

That's funny, I thinks. Why does **Duck**
sound so muffled? I is not understanding
a word he is saying.

"You'll have to speak up, **Duck**," I says.
"I don't thinks my imagination is working
very well."

"Um hot hin hur hemagination. Hum hin
he hool hox hon he Hocket!"

Duck sounded like he is shouting, but I still has no idea what he is saying. This must be one of his funny games, I thinks. So I plays along.

"Hut har hu hoing in he hool hox," I says.

"Um huck han ham hying hue het hout!" Duck replies.

"Hu har herry hunny, huck in he hool hox. Ha! Ha! Ha!" **Duck** is so silly.

"Pig! You big banana! I'm not huck in the hool hox! I am stuck in the toolbox!"

Now **Duck's** voice is super clear. I opens my eyes and looks out of the window, down at the toolbox stuck on the side of the Trocket. I can just see **Duck's** yellow beak

poking out of a little gap.

I is so excited that **Duck** is here with me that I forgets about the EVIL SPACE ALIENS and goes outside to let **Duck** out of the toolbox.

I is SOOOOOO happy to see him and I thinks he is very happy to see me. I is really wanting to give him the biggest hug ever, but I thinks if I do, then I would squish him flat and then I would be back to being on my own on Pluto without my bestest friend and that would be BAD!

Duck told me that he decided he would rather be lost in space with me, than staying back on the farm without me.

He was not liking the thought of me being scared and alone, so he hid in the toolbox and came to make sure I was OK. When **Duck** tells me this it makes me love him even more. But I don't tell him that 'cause that would make me sound like a Softie Pig. So I tells **Duck** he is so silly. I is a Brave Pig, I is not scared of anything . . . well, apart from the **SPACE ALIENS**.

I points them out to **Duck** and whispers, just in case they can hear me, that I thinks they might be evil.

Duck looks at them and starts laughing. **"Don't be silly, Pig, they're not evil—they're gardin-noams."**

I is thinking that "gardin-noams" must be a funny **Duck** word for "nice."

"How do you know the **SPACE ALIENS** is gardin-noams?" I says. **Duck** is the silly one. How can he be so sure they is nice?

He hasn't even spoken to them.

Duck laughs even more. I looks again at the **SPACE ALIENS** and STILL they is doing nothing. I is sure they is EVIL!

"I know they are gardin-noams, Pig, because Farmer has one in his garden!"

Suddenly my head feels very muddled. Farmer has a **SPACE ALIEN** in his garden and **Duck** has met it!! Why hasn't he told me this before? Has **Farmer** been to Pluto?

Duck explains to me that they is

Garden Gnomes—not a funny **Duck** word but small things that **Farmers** keep in their gardens. **Duck** says they is "**ornyments**." I tells **Duck** I is still confused. I don't understand what ornyments is doing on Pluto.

Then **Duck** says the most bonkers thing. He says we is not in space. We is back on Earth.

"On Earth?" I says.

"We landed in a different sort of Pluto. We've landed in William H. Pluto Garden Center, it says so on that sign on top of the big shed over there. I think the sat nav must have gotten a bit confused up there in space and brought us here instead of the real Pluto."

Duck says he thinks that we might not be too far from the Farm. He says he saw **Mrs. Farmer** taking some bags out of her car the other day with the same writing on them as what is on the sign. For a teeny-tiny moment I is very excited. If we is near the Farm, then we is near slops! GOOD! GOOD! GOOD! But then I suddenly remembers that if we is near the Farm, we

is also near **Farmer** and that is BAD!
BAD! BAD! What if **Mr.** and **Mrs.**
Farmer come here and find me? They
will take me back to the farm and
chip-chop me up for sausages.

AHHHHH HHHH!

Duck says it is important not to panic. He says we should find a safe place to hide and make a plan.

Just next to the Garden Gnomes is some big orange pots that is upside down. **Duck** says these is giant flowerpots and they will be perfect to hide under and think.

I lifts up the edge of the biggest one and **Duck** slides inside. It is not so easy for me 'cause I is quite a bit bigger. I reverses in, bottom first. I wiggles and waggles backwards while **Duck** helps me the best he can by pulling my tail. Finally we is both under the flowerpot. It is a very tight squeeze. Duck lies on top of me so we can both fit in. We is both super tired. **Duck**

falls asleep and I is writing to you in my diary before I dozes off myself. I is very happy to be back on Earth, even though horrible **Mr.** and **Mrs. Farmer** is not so far away.

whizzleday

Hello.

I has made a very important decision. Even though I is back on Earth, I is still going to make up my own name days. I thinks this is much more fun. I hopes you agree.

Today was quite a bonkers day. I has so much to tell you, so here goes.

When we wakes up from our little sleep, we starts to try and make a plan. **Duck** says we can't stay in the Garden Center:

1. Because **Mr.** and **Mrs. Farmer** might find me here and take me home and eat me.

2. Because any **Farmer** might find me here and take me home and eat me. **Duck** says **Farmers** like eating Pigs. He says they also like eating **Ducks** too. Wow! **Farmers** really can be super evil. Why would they want to eat **Duck**?

Duck says he thinks our best option is to refuel the Trocket and use it to fly somewhere else. He says he is not sure where yet, but he is sure we will figure it out—anywhere is better than a place jam-packed full of **Farmers**. I just hopes it is somewhere with lots of yummy slops.

To make fuel I needs to eat. **Duck** poo is too small and too runny to make good fuel, so it is all up to me and my bottom. **Duck** says he thinks there might be food in the big shed with the sign on top. **Farmers** always keeps food in sheds.

When we comes out from under the flowerpot, I sees the Garden Center for the first time in daylight. **Duck** says Garden Centers is where **Farmers** come to get things to make their gardens look nice. I is very confused why a **Farmer** would want a big stone **Farmer** with Chicken wings blowing water out of his ears, or a giant **Frog** blowing water out of its bottom. **Duck** says they is called "water fountains." I says they is silly!

The Trocket is way too big for us to hide, but I is thinking that it does not look stranger than all the other weird ornyments and fountains that is all around. Duck says he hopes I is right because we has to leave it where it is while we goes off to find slops.

We creeps as carefully as we can towards the big shed.

We is just tiptoeing through a bit that is full of wooden ornyments when we spots a different **Mr.** and **Mrs. Farmer** and a **mini-farmer**. I is guessing the

mini-farmer is belonging to the **Mr.** and **Mrs. Farmer**. He is very fat and waddles like **Duck** does. The **Mr.** and **Mrs. Farmer** is looking at some flowers. The **mini-farmer** looks bored. He comes over to where me and **Duck** is. **Duck** whispers to stand super still and try and look like ornyments. We both stands as still as we can.

The **mini-farmer** picks up a wooden **Sheep** ornyment that is standing near us and pulls its head off. He laughs and throws it on the floor. Then he picks up a wooden **COW** and does the same. What an evil

mini-farmer! I is thinking you would not be liking him either. He then walks over to **Duck** and bends over to pick him up. There is no way I is going to let him try and pull **Duck's** head off. As he bends over I bites him as hard as I can on his fat bottom. I digs my teeth right into his soft and squidgy bum. Evil **mini-farmer** makes a terrible howling noise. I lets go of his bottom and he runs back to the **Mr.** and **Mrs. Farmer** screaming and crying. He points at us but we stands super, super still. **Mr.** and **Mrs. Farmer** looks angry with him and drags him off.

Ha! Ha! Evil **mini-farmer**, you is not going to hurt my best friend!!!!

Duck says I should be very proud of myself for being so brave. This makes me feel happy inside. Maybe I isn't a Softie Pig after all.

Finally we makes it to the doors of the big shed. They is huge—they makes me feel very small. But I is being brave so I says to **Duck**, "Don't worry, I will open them," even though I is really not sure how I can. But I doesn't even have to try. When I gets up to them they opens with a big

WHOOOOSH noise. I has no idea how I did it but I is not going to tell **Duck** that. I just pretends like I knew exactly what I was doing.

The shed is huge inside and full of all sorts of strange things. The things I likes the most is called a Sit-on Lawn Mower. They looks like little tractors. If I was a **Farmer**, I would have one of these and ride around on it all day long.

There is not any **Farmer** in the big shed, so we don't have to do any more pretending to be ornyments.

Just past the Sit-on Lawn Mowers we comes to this bit that is full of bags with pictures of animals on them. They is just like the bags that **Farmer** feeds the **Sheep** with, only they don't have pictures of **Sheep** on them, they has pictures of **Dogs** and Cats. There is even some small boxes with pictures of orange **Fishies** on them. I

 is so hungry I don't cares whose food is inside.

I pulls one off the shelf with a picture of a **Dog** on it. We don't

have any special **Farmer** tools to open it, so I uses my big bottom. I does a little jump in the air and lands right in the middle of it. Bang goes the bag and all these brown biscuit things fly out everywhere. Woo-hoo! Food!

But the food tastes DISGUSTING! It is horrible and dry and it makes me cough. Cough! Cough! Cough! I is very glad I  **YUCK!** is not a **Dog**! I tries another bag, with a picture of a Cat on it, but that is horrible and dry too. And the little orange **Fishie** food is the worst of all. I tells **Duck** I is not sure I can eat enough of this to make the poo we need. **Duck** says he has an idea.

Next to the shed with all the bags of food is a small pond with little **Fishies** in it. **Duck** says if we pour all the biscuits into the pond and mix them up, they will be easier to eat. They'll be just like slops. So we opens lots of bags and pours them all in. Then I gets in and mixes them all up. **Duck** is right. It's gloopy, just like slops. And it tastes yummy, just like slops. HOORAH! I is so happy, I gobbles it all up until there is nothing left.

Not even the little **Fishies** ... OOOOOOPs!

Duck says I is as round as a hay bale. Ha! Ha! A Pig Bale. I feels like I might go pop at any second.

I wishes that we could just go back to the Trocket, fill it with poo, and fly away from here. But we can't because it takes me a little while to turn slops into poo. So we goes and hides back under the big flowerpot and waits while my tummy goes gurgle, gurgle, gurgle. **Duck** says we should have a little sleep so we has lots of energy for when we is flying. So that is what we is going to do.

whizzleday (part two)

Hello.

As I was lying waiting for my tummy to turn all the slops into poo, this thought pops into my head.

I loves the Farm. The Farm is my home. But we can't go there because **Mr.** and **Mrs. Farmer** is there and they wants to eat me up. And the EVIL CHICKENS are there and they is evil and nasty. But if we could make **Mr.** and **Mrs. Farmer** and the EVIL CHICKENS not there, then it would be the best place in the whole world to be.

I whispers my idea to **Duck**. I think he is a little surprised that I has had such a good one. He says it is great. I feels very, very proud. No one has ever said my ideas is great before.

I was just about to tell him the best bit, how I thinks we can make them all not there (I is very pleased with this bit), when we heard loud **Farmer** voices.

Duck says they was talking about the Trocket. I hears a very high, squeaky-sounding **Farmer**. I is thinking that this must be the evil **mini-farmer** that tried to pull **Duck's** head off earlier.

Duck listens to what they is saying. He says it is not good. The evil **mini-farmer** wants the Trocket to play with in his garden.

I is not going to let him get our Trocket! We has to do something fast. **Duck** agrees. So we carefully wiggles out from underneath the flowerpot. Luckily **Mr.** and **Mrs. Farmer** and the evil **mini-farmer** are standing on the other side of the Trocket, so they can't see us. Quiet as we can, we climbs up inside the Trocket. I sits on my special seat and starts to fill up the fuel tank with poo, while **Duck** keeps an eye on the **Farmers**.

I tries to be as quick and as quiet as I can. But when I poos, I always farts. I bets you does too? It's only little ones but the evil **mini-farmer** hears them and looks straight up at us. I sits as still as I can, pretending to be an ornyment again. But I thinks he must have remembered that it was me that bit his bottom. He starts shouting and pointing. They all looks up to where **Duck** and I is sitting.

Then **Mr. Farmer** reaches up and opens the Trocket door. Me and **Duck** looks at each other. He looks as scared as I feel. The **mini-farmer** jumps up onto the Trocket's steps and starts climbing up towards us.

I does the only thing that I knows how to: I lets out a MASSIVE fart. It's a real stinker. It smells of orange **Fishies'** food and **Cats'** food and **Dogs'** food all mixed together. The **mini-farmer** almost falls off the steps, it's that bad. They all hold their noses and start coughing.

I has no more time to make any more poo fuel. While they is coughing away, **Duck** jumps out and presses the big green GO button on the side of the Trocket.

The Trocket roars into life and all the **Farmers** jump backwards to get out of the way of the flames.

They looks very surprised. The evil **mini-farmer** tries to grab **Duck**, but **Duck** is too quick and scrambles up the wheel away from his evil **mini-farmer** hands.

The Trocket doesn't shoot up into the air like it did before. It stays on the ground, just shaking and shuddering and making a loud *putt-putt-putt* noise. A Picken voice says, "OH YOU SILLY, SILLY PIGGY-WIGGY! THE FUEL IS MUCH TOO LOW FOR FLIGHT MODE. DRIVE MODE WILL NOW ACTIVATE. GOOD LUCK, OLD CHAP, YOU REALLY WILL NEED IT! KLA! KLA! KLA!"

Suddenly the Trocket falls forward so now it is on all four wheels and I realize what is happening. I is going to have to drive. BUT I CAN'T DRIVE.

I IS A PIG

AND

PIGS DON'T
DRIVE!!!!

But it's too late to stop. The Trocket shoots off across the Garden Center, leaving the **Mr.** and **Mrs. Farmer** and their evil **mini-farmer** in a cloud of smelly poo smoke.

I doesn't know what to do. I looks for **Duck**, but **Duck** is clinging on to the side of the Trocket. The evil **mini-farmer** runs after us, still trying to grab him. I quickly winds down the window with the trotter I is

not steering with, grabs hold of one of **Duck's** wings, and pulls him back into the Trocket.

We crashes through the Garden Gnomes, the water fountains, and the wooden animal ornyments, and straight out through the front gates. Bye, bye, evil **mini-farmer**. You can't run as fast as our Trocket!

I tries to press the brake to slow us down a little, because it is very hard to control the Trocket when it is going so fast. But my leg is not long enough to reach it. So we is stuck going

FAAAAAASSSST!

Duck says I has to try and steer the Trocket so that it stays on the big gray path that he calls a "road." I tries my best to do this, but it is not easy. The silly road has silly bendy bits in it. I finds them very difficult. It is much easier to drive straight across them than around them.

We is out of control.

We crashes through fences and hedges. We even goes through something that **Duck** says is called a Villidge Hall. There were lots of **Farmers** in it, having a big party. I did a little wave as we drove through, to try and be polite. I thinks we might have been making quite a big mess.

OOOoOPs!

Duck presses some buttons on the sat nav. He says that because this is **Farmer's**

sat nav, it will know the way to get back to where **Farmer** lives. He says it is super clever. It's also still super rude.

It says, "PLEASE TURN YOUR FAT LITTLE PIGGY FACE TO THE LEFT AT THE RAMP, RIGHT AT THE INTERSECTION, AND STRAIGHT OVER THE ROUNDABOUT. KLA! KLA! KLA! KLA! KLA!"

Duck points so I don't have to take my eyes off the road to look at the sat nav. When we gets to the rownderbought he tells me to go around it. But I don't know how, so I steers straight and we flies over the big bump in the middle.

Wheeeeeeee!

I is starting to get the hang of this, I thinks. I feels like Pig the Race-Trocket Driver.

Now the road is getting thinner and thinner and the hedges is getting taller and taller. This makes driving a bit easier 'cause if you go wrong, the hedges bounce you back the way you need to

go. Bounce! Bounce! Bounce! It's great fun.
I is not sure that **Duck** thinks it is quite
as fun as I does 'cause he goes a very funny
green color. "Don't worry, **Duck**, I is sure
we will be there soon," I says. Bounce!
Bounce! Bounce!

We is bouncing along happily when I sees
another tractor coming down the road
towards us. The other tractor stops when
it sees us. But we can't stop. **Duck** screams,

"AHHHHHHHHH!"

and I screams,

"AHHHHHHHHHH!"

and I thinks, as we get close, I can see the
Farmer in the other tractor scream

"AHHHHHHHHH!"

I guess he has never seen a Pig driving a Trocket before. Ha! Ha!

Right at the very last minute I spies a gateway. I turns the steering wheel and we smashes through the gate and rockets off across the field. Whew—whee! I is very pleased with myself. I is sure **Duck** is quite pleased with me too, but he can't tell me 'cause he too busy going greener and greener.

Driving in fields is much easier than driving on roads. You don't have to worry about going around silly corners. The sat nav says all we has to do to reach the

Farm is "MAY WE KINDLY SUGGEST YOU
BEAR RIGHT AT THE OLD OAK TREE, MAKE A
HARD RIGHT AT THE RIVER, AND TAKE THE
THIRD EXIT AT THE RUSTY OLD DIGGER, YOU
OVERSIZED PINK WINDBAG. KLA! KLA! KLA!
KLA! KLA!"

As we whizzes across the field that
Farmer keeps his big hay pile in, I
suddenly realize I is not sure how we is
going to stop. We is getting very close to
the Farm and I don't want **Farmer**
to hear us or see us. We has no option. I
has to stop the Trocket somehow. So I
turns the steering wheel around as hard
as I can and we spins around and drives
straight back towards the big haystack.

"HOLD ON TIGHT!!"

I shouts to **Duck**.

WHUUUMPPP!

We go straight into the haystack. The front of the Trocket disappears completely inside. It makes spluttering noise and stops. Phew! We has made it!

Duck says that he is very glad the journey is over and that he never wants to drive anywhere with me again. **Duck** is so rude sometimes!

We decides to sleep in the Trocket tonight 'cause **Duck** is afraid that if we

sleeps outside **Fox** might come and gobble him up. We can't go back to the Farm 'cause if we go there **Farmer** will gobble me up.

So I lies on the seat and **Duck** lies on top of me. **Duck** says I make a very comfy bed, though he says he wishes his bed didn't have such a noisy tummy.

Phew! That was a lot to write. My trotter is super tired and achy. I really hopes that you enjoys reading it all.

Zabberday

Hello.

This morning I wakes up early, excited to tell **Duck** about the next bit of my plan. I is even prouder of this bit than I was of the first bit. My plan is to trick **Mr.** and **Mrs. Farmer** and all the EVIL CHICKENS into the Trocket and blast them off into space. I is sure that **Duck** is going to be super impressed when he hears this. So I wakes him up and I is just telling him about it when the Trocket starts to rock from side to side. At first it is just rocking a little, and then it gets more and more until it is swaying.

"Silly itchy Sheep," says **Duck**.

We both looks out of the window and, sure enough, the Trocket is surrounded by lots of **Sheeps** all rubbing themselves up and down against the Trocket. **Sheeps** is always itchy. This is because they is covered in wool and wool is very itchy. I is very glad I is not a **Sheep**.

Duck opens the Trocket door and all the **Sheeps** jump back. **Sheeps** is quite big Scaredy-Cats too. He is just about to be saying something to them when, with a huge shake and a terrible creaking noise, the Trocket falls apart. Just like that, the wheels all pop off, the doors fall out, and the rocket drops to the ground. **Duck** and I is left sitting on the tractor seat, surrounded by

bits of tractor and rocket. The silly **Sheeps** has messed up my best ever idea. There is no way we can use the Trocket now!

The **Sheeps** don't even notice what they has done. They just continue scratching themselves up against the rocket.

Duck says not to worry, he thinks that the **Sheeps** might have done us a favor. I says I is not sure how itching the Trocket to pieces is doing us a favor. "**Well**," he says, "**now we can attach the rocket to whatever we like. For example, we could attach it to the Chicken House. Just wait until Mr. and Mrs. Farmer come to collect the eggs and then *whoooooshhhh*! We send them all off into space.**"

"A Chicken House Rocket! A Chocket!"
I says. "Great!" **Duck** is so clever. I don't
understand why I is not as clever, 'cause
my head is much, much bigger than his.

All we need to do now is work out how
we is going to get the rocket to the
Chicken House. **Duck** points at the **Sheeps**,
who is still itching themselves on the
rocket. Every time they rubs themselves
on it they rolls it around. The **Sheeps** can
help us move it! Perfect. Well, nearly
perfect. We has to get the **Sheeps** to
agree to help us, and **Sheeps**, along with
being itchy and a bit scaredy, is also
very lazy.

Duck, who speaks **Sheeps**, stands on top

of one of the tractor's wheels and calls to them.

"Morning, Sheeps," says **Duck,** "itchy **baaaaaaaacks?"**

"Yaaaaaar," they all says back in one big voice. **Sheeps** does everything together, even talking. **Sheeps** is a very easy language to understand 'cause they is too lazy to use many words. If I listens very carefully, even I can understands what they is saying.

"Can you help us move thiiiiiis over thaaaaaaaar?" Duck says, pointing towards the yard.

"Naaaaaaaar," they all says, shaking their heads.

"If you do it, Pig will give you all an

extra-big baaaaaaaack scraaaaaatch," Duck

says, winking at me.

I gives **Duck** a big evil stare. I don't want to give ALL the **Sheeps** an extra big back scratch. Why can't **Duck** give them a back scratch? But this idea seems to make the **Sheeps** change their mind, so I shuts up.

"Yaaaaaaaaaar," they all says. "**Ohhhhhh, yaaaaaaaaaar!**"

And they all rushes over to me and makes a line. So, one by one, I can give them all a scratch.

Duck finds it all very funny. I find

it all very NOT funny. **Sheeps** is more woolly than I had ever imagined. As I scratches them, little balls of their wool comes off. It gets stuck all over me. **Duck** says I looks like I is turning into a **Sheep**.

Suddenly I has another one of my brilliant disguise ideas. I think this one might be even better than the stack of hay and a pile of poo ideas. If I covers myself in wool, then **Mr.** and **Mrs.**

Farmer will thinks I is a **Sheep**, so even if they spots me, they will never know it is me. How smart is that!!!

I gives each **Sheep** the biggest back scratch I can so lots of wool comes off. The **Sheeps** has so much they doesn't even notice. It takes me a very long time to scratch the whole flock, but when I finally finishes I has made a gigantic woolly pile that is nearly as tall as me.

I finds a puddle of mud and rolls around in it, then I goes back to the pile of wool and I rolls around and around in that. By the time I is finished, I is covered from head to toe in wool. Boy, oh boy, is it very, very itchy!

Duck and I sits on the hill and waits for the sun to go down. We has to wait till it is nighttime so **Mr.** and **Mrs. Farmer** will be fast asleep and won't see us.

As I looks at the Farm I gets a funny feeling in my tummy. I is a little bit scared. OK, if I is honest with you, I is a lot scared. I can see **Farmer's Shed**, the one he wants to chip-chop me up in. The gold metal square with the sad-faced fat pig on it shines in the sunlight, giving me goose bumps just like it did the first time I saw it. If our plan doesn't work, I will end up in there and I will never see **Duck** again. In fact, I won't see anything ever again. I starts to shake a little.

I must be shaking more than I think 'cause **Duck** says, "**What's wrong, Pig? Are you scared?**"

"Who, me?" I says. "Don't be so silly. I is not scared. I is just a bit cold."

I is not sure that Duck is believing me. I is, after all, wearing a big woolly coat.

But he doesn't say nothing 'cause I don't think he wants to embarrass me. He really is my very best friend. And when you has your best friend with you, you stops feeling scared and you starts feeling a bit more brave. We can do this, I thinks.

YES, WE CAN!

Bingo Night

Hello.

When I has told you that things that have happened has been bonkers, well they has never been as bonkers as what happened tonight. What happened tonight is much more bonkers than all the bonkers that I has ever said was bonkers. Wow! That's a lot of bonkers. I is starting to go bonkers just writing bonkers so many times. Anyways, here is what happened.

Finally as the sun started to set, the **Sheeps** stood in a big circle around the rocket and slowly started to itch it across the field. I stood among them,

pretending to be a **Sheep**. **Duck** walked in front and gave directions. By the time we reaches the gate into the yard the sun has totally gone and the bright stars and moon are all we has to help us see our way.

As we slowly pushes the rocket into the yard I clearly sees **Farmer's Shed**, but I don't feel scared inside no more. I feels sort of excited inside. I knows what we has to do. I just wants to go on and do it.

The first thing we has to do is get the rocket over to the big poo heap and fill it as full as we can with poo so it will go as far into space as possible. **Duck** points the **Sheeps** in the direction of the heap, but they is so busy having a nice time scratching that they scratches the rocket right past the poo heap and off towards the Old Hay Barn.

The **Sheeps** are out of control. **Duck** and me has to run around and, using all our strength, push their woolly bottoms in the direction we want them to go. Off the rocket goes, flying back towards the poo heap. Luckily this time they pushes the rocket right into it, so it can't go any

farther. Me and **Duck** quickly scrambles up
to the top of the heap and starts filling it
up super full with stinking poo. The **Sheeps**
continue to busily scratch away. **Duck** tells
the **Sheeps** not to itch against the GO
button in case the rocket accidentally
takes off. That would be very BAD!

We then gets the **Sheeps** to push the
rocket over to the Chicken House. The
Sheeps is not very accurate, and me and
Duck has to push and shove them in the
right direction so that they don't itch
the rocket into **COW shed** by mistake.
I is not wanting **COW** to rocket off into
space. **COW** is way too nice and full
of yummy milk.

As we gets closer to the **CHICKEN HOUSE** I can hear the sound of the **EVIL CHICKENS'** evil snoring: "**ZNORE, ZNORE, ZNORE.**"

ZNORE!
ZNORE!
ZNORE!
ZNORE!

Luckily the **Sheeps** is getting tired and slowing down so we can control where the rocket is going more easily. With a final wiggle and a waggle we gets the rocket into position.

Duck tells the **Sheeps** they can stop. I thinks they would liked to have itched themselves on the rocket forever. They all turns and looks at me. I knows what they is thinking. They is thinking they wants another piggy back scratch. I shakes my head. No way is I doing that again. **Duck** quietly reminds them that there are lots of bits of old tractor in the field that they can go and scratch themselves on. This does the trick. They all turns and scuttles out of the yard and back up to the field.

We is left all alone, just me, **Duck**, and the poo-filled rocket. We put the final touches to our plan. We pushes some dirt and soil from the yard up against the rocket so **Farmer** won't notice it. All we has to do now is wait until morning for **Mr.** and **Mrs. Farmer** to come and collect the eggs. How exciting, I thinks. This is going to work!

And then I goes and ruins it all.

It's not a very big fart that I lets out, just a little excited one, but it is very, very smelly. (You know how sometimes the small ones can be the worst.) It is so smelly that it wakes the EVIL CHICKENS. Before I even has a chance to hide, one of them slides open the door. It's the SUPER EVIL one. It looks right at me with its evil black eyes and says, "WELL, WELL, WELL, WHAT ON EARTH DO WE HAVE HERE? A SHEEP THAT SMELLS LIKE A PIG. I DO BELIEVE THAT IS YOU, SMELLY-WELLY PIGGY-WIGGY, IN ANOTHER OF YOUR STUPID DISGUISES."

"No," I says, trying to stop my voice

from shaking. I can't believe they know it is me. "I is not Pig. I is a **Sheep!**"

"IF YOU ARE A SHEEP, MY DEAR BOY, WHY ARE YOU SPEAKING PIG?"

Oh no, how silly of me! All the other **EVIL CHICKENS** poke their heads out and stare.

"OH DEARY ME, YOU SILLY PIGGY-WIGGY. WE HAVE BEEN EXPECTING YOU. WE SAW

YOU GO ALL THE WAY INTO SPACE AND
THEN STUPIDLY TURN AROUND AND COME
ALL THE WAY BACK DOWN TO EARTH. WE
SAW IT THROUGH OUR TELESCOPE. YOU
REALLY ARE THE STUPIDEST CREATURE
IN THE WHOLE WIDE WORLD."

I starts to argue that it wasn't my

fault, it was the
stupid sat nav's.
But the EVIL CHICKENS
don't care.

"WELL, IT MAKES
NO DIFFERENCE
NOW. YOU ARE BACK
AND YOU KNOW HOW

PLEASED THE Farmer WILL BE TO SEE

YOU. CHIPPY-CHOPPY-UPPY PIGGY-WIGGY.
KLA! KLA! KLA! KLA! KLA! KLA! KLA! KLA!"

I is not knowing what to say. Our clever
plan has gone totally wrong
and it's all my fault. I feels
tears start to fill up my
eyes. I doesn't want to
die in that horrible shed.
I looks around for **Duck**,
but in the dark I
can't see him.

"OH DEARY, DEARY ME, THE PIG IS
CRYING. KLA! KLA! KLA! KLA!" They all
starts to pretend wipe their evil eyes with
their wings. I feels my heart drop to the
very bottom of my tummy.

Then all of a sudden I hears **Duck** cry out, "**Fox! Fox! Fox! Heading for the Chicken House!**"

Like I told you before, **Fox** is the only thing the **EVIL CHICKENS** is scared of. They all

stops looking at me, starts clucking and squawking in panic, and rushes back into their house and slams the door.

Duck runs over to me, still quacking as loud as he can, "**Fox! Fox! He's coming!**"

"Oh, no!" I says, realizing. "You has to hide! I don't want him to eats you up too."

"**Don't be silly, Pig,**" whispers **Duck**. "**There is no Fox, but we have to make the Evil Chickens think there is.**"

I see a light come on over in the Farmhouse. **Farmer** is awake! I starts to panic even more.

"**It's OK, Pig, we just need to change the plan,**" **Duck** says. "**We can't wait till morning anymore. We have to get Mr. and Mrs. Farmer into the CHICKEN HOUSE right now. Farmer loves his CHICKENS. He won't let Fox eat them all up.**"

Now I is understanding! **Farmer** will come to save the EVIL CHICKENS. **Duck** is so clever.

In the distance I hears the thud of footsteps and then bang! **Farmer** and **Mrs. Farmer** come flying out of the front door. They runs straight towards us. **"As soon as they step inside the CHICKEN HOUSE, you shut the door,"** **Duck** says, **"and I'll start the rocket."**

Duck quickly disappears into the dark. Now I'm standing alone.

My legs go all wibbly-wobbly. All I can think is, what if **Farmer** isn't fooled by my disguise either? He will take me into his shed and I will never, ever come out. My heart starts to pound so hard I can't even hear their footsteps as they runs across the yard. Before I knows it they is right next to me.

Boom!
Boom!
Boom!

goes my heart. It is so loud I is worried they will hear it too. I is too scared to look at them. I just looks at the floor and does the only thing I can thinks of. I goes, "Baaaaaaaaaar."

Farmer mutters something that sounds like, "**Get out my way, Sheep!**" He gives me a big shove and they both charge on towards the **CHICKEN HOUSE**. Ha! Ha! Ha! **EVIL CHICKENS**, you is wrong. My disguise is very good after all!

Mr. and **Mrs. Farmer** runs up the little steps that leads to the **CHICKEN HOUSE**, opens the door, and goes inside.

I runs up the steps after them, closes the door, and presses my big bottom as hard as I can against it, so **Mr.** and **Mrs. Farmer** can't open it and get out.

I looks down at **Duck**. He gives me a little nod and then presses the big green GO button on the side of the rocket.

ROOOAAAARRR!

The rocket comes to life. Flames fire out of it. The power of rocket slowly starts

to pull the legs of the **CHICKEN HOUSE** out
of the ground.

Mr. and **Mrs. Farmer** and the **EVIL
CHICKENS** pushes hard against the door,
trying to get out. I knows I can't let
them. But there is lots of them and only
one of me, and just like that BAM! The
door is open and I is lying on my back at

the bottom of the steps. **Mr.** and **Mrs. Farmer** both tries to squeeze out of the small door at once.

This can't happen, I thinks. They can't escape and chip-chop me into little pieces and eat me.

"**Fart!**" I hear **Duck** shout over the noise of the rocket. "**Fart! Pig! Fart now!!!**"

I has no idea why **Duck** wants me to do this, but I has no time to asks why. I does the biggest fart I can.

PAAAAAAA RRRRRP!

And then the most amazing thing ever happens: The flames from the rocket catch it on fire.

Huge flames fire out of my bottom and up towards **Mr.** and **Mrs. Farmer**. They stops trying to escape and holds their hands up to their faces to protect themselves from my fart flames.

The fart flames also burns off all my

wool. I sees **Farmer** look down at me.
I is covered in black soot and the little
bits of wool still stuck to me are smoking.
I is no longer a **Sheep**. I is a Pig again—well,
a smoking, black-colored Pig. **Farmer**
rubs his eyes. I is not sure he believes what
he is seeing.

"**Pig?**" I

hears him say.

"**Roast Pig?**"

For a tiny

moment I

remembers how

much I used to love **Farmer**, how

happy I was when he called me my special

name. Then just like that

WHOOMMPPHHH!

the wooden legs pull out of the ground

and the Chocket rockets off.

"Good-bye!" I says and gives him a

little wave.

Duck and I watches until the Chocket

looks like just another star in the sky. Good-bye, **Mr.** and **Mrs. Farmer**. Good-bye, **EVIL CHICKENS**. I hopes you finds somewhere nice to live in space and never, ever, comes back!!!

Yabberday

Hello.

It is a couple of days since I has written to you. That is because I has been very busy eating. I has eaten:

1. All the vegetables in **Farmer's** vegetable patch.

2. All the corn in the corn shed (**Duck** helped a bit).

3. All the old slops in **Mr.** and **Mrs. Farmer's** garbage cans.

4. All the slops in the cold white mini-shed in **Mr.** and **Mrs. Farmer's** house—some of the slops in there was so cold it made my head hurt when I ate them.

5. All the slops that **Mr.** and **Mrs. Farmer** keeps in little metal tins. Getting them out was great fun. I simply jumps on the tin and all the yummy slops flies out everywhere. Then I goes around and licks it all up—yummmmmmy!

6. All the special

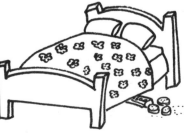

biscuits that I found next to **Mrs. Farmer's** bed. **Farmer's** biscuits are much more tasty than animal biscuits!

I tried not to eat everything, to save some slops for laters, but once I started I couldn't stop. It was all too yummy. I thinks maybe I has been a very silly Pig, 'cause now I has nothing to eat but yucky, yucky grass.

I goes over to **Duck Pond** and I tells **Duck** how much I misses my slops. **Duck** says he kind of misses his corn. **COW** is getting a bit bored of hay too. I says that I wishes there was such a thing as a **nice Farmer**, a **Farmer** who wouldn't want to eat me or **Duck** up, and who would take care of **COW** and all the **Sheeps**. **Duck** says that there is. They is called **Vegytarian Farmers** and they only likes eating vegytables. He says that they looks just like **Mr.** and **Mrs. Farmer**, only instead of boots like **Mr.** and **Mrs. Farmer** wore, they wears things that is called sandals and they has very long hair.

I is very excited when I is hearing this. I bet if they likes vegytables, likes I does, then they will know how to make the best slops EVER!!!

I shows **Duck** my Top Secret Diary (only best friends is allowed to see things that is top secret) and I says why don't we leave it at the Villidge Hall where we saw all the **Farmers**. I is sure there must be some **Farmer** that can understand Pig. They can read all about our big adventures and how we now need to find a **Vegytarian Farmer** to come and take care of us.

Duck is finding my diary very funny. I says it is not funny; it is top secret. **Duck** says it should be called the "Unbelievable Top Secret Diary," 'cause no one is really going to believe that all these things happened to us. I likes the word "unbelievable" 'cause it makes me looks likes I is knowing really big long words. **Duck** also says I should draw a special map, so the **Vegytarian Farmer** knows where to find us.

If you is reading this right now, then our plan has worked: My Unbelievable Top Secret diary has made it to you. Hopefully you knows a **Vegytarian Farmer** or, even better, maybe you is a **Vegytarian Farmer**.

I really hopes you can help 'cause grass is yucky and I is missing my slops VERY much!

Look, I has drawn a map for you.

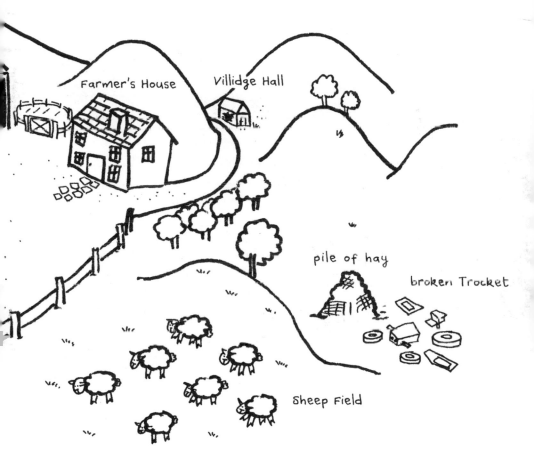

Farmer's House

Villidge Hall

pile of hay

broken Trocket

Sheep Field

Lots of love,

Pig, **Duck,**

COW,

and all the

Sheeps

XXXX